Dedicated to Summer, Sachin and Mandy,
in loving memory of Dean

My sister Trace wrote *Shine* for my children, Summer and Sachin, soon after their father's
sudden death. In the face of a terrible tragedy and a loss so enormous it seemed we could barely
breathe, the story of *Shine* was a moment of peace and beauty that helped a little in explaining the
inexplicable. It is a story based on the great love my husband and I shared with each other and for
our children, a story of hope that inspired me to carry on, and a story of family – of my children and
me as well as my sister and the compassion she was able to show us through her words and pictures.
I will be forever grateful to her for creating such a beautiful gift, which she and I hope
others may also gain some comfort from.

MANDY BALLA-KELLETT, 2015

My Granny Hitchcock used to say, 'We all come from the stars, we all go back to the stars…'
That's what my sister, Mandy, told her children that terrible day. That's where this story
comes from – and from the very bottom of my heart, for them.

TRACE BALLA, 2015

shine

Trace Balla

ALLEN&UNWIN

SYDNEY · MELBOURNE · AUCKLAND · LONDON

Far, far away and long, long ago,
on a beautiful planet, amongst the golden stars,
there lived a young horse.

He was so kind and bright,
so sparkly and shimmery,
that everyone called him Shine.

He grew up to be an amazing horse.

He loved to gallop with the other horses
under the smiling moon.

One day Shine saw some hoofprints in the sand.
They belonged to Glitter. She was the loveliest horse
he'd ever seen.

Together they galloped under the golden sun.

One night a sparkle came down from a star,
and then another, right into their hearts.

The sparkles grew into two playful little horses
called Shimmer and Sparky.

What a joyful time they all had.

But every horse has to go back to its star some day.
And one day it was Shine's turn to go.

'I'm so sorry. I don't feel like going, but my time has come.
I love you all so much,' he said.

And then he went to join the other stars
up in the beautiful, sparkling night sky.

That night everything seemed so dark. And Glitter was
so sad that Shine had gone. She started to cry…
and out of her eyes came golden tears.

'Why are your tears golden?' asked Sparky.

'Because my love for your daddy is golden,' said Glitter.

All through the long dark night, she cried and cried.
The little horses cried golden tears, too.
By morning, they had made a huge golden ocean.

'I wonder how big our ocean is?' said Shimmer.

'Shall we climb that mountain to see?' said Glitter.

They walked and walked until they reached
the highest mountain. It was so big and so steep
that Glitter wasn't sure if she could climb it.

'You can do it,' said Shimmer and Sparky.

And they stepped off her back
and walked beside her.

When they reached the very top of the mountain,
they saw a vast golden ocean.

'That's how much love we have for each other,' said Glitter.
'As much as there could possibly be.'

And they were all amazed.

Reflected in the golden ocean were
thousands and thousands of sparkling stars.

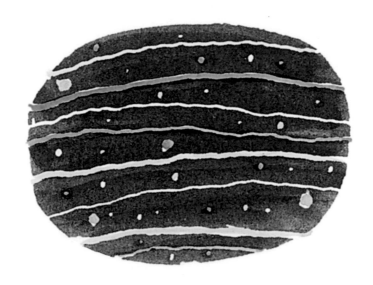

And when they looked up into the sky,
there, shining brightest of all, was their special star,
the star called Shine.

This was their daddy's star,
looking down on them, shining its bright,
golden light onto them and into their hearts,
for ever and ever.

'It's late now,' said Glitter. 'It's been such
a big day, climbing up the mountain.'

So they curled up together and closed their eyes.

The stars shone down on them,
and they slept a deep and beautiful sleep.

First published in Australia in 2015 by Allen & Unwin
First published in the United Kingdom in 2015 by Allen & Unwin

Allen & Unwin – Australia
83 Alexander Street, Crows Nest NSW 2065, Australia
Phone: (61 2) 8425 0100
Email: info@allenandunwin.com
Web: www.allenandunwin.com

Allen & Unwin – UK
c/o Murdoch Books, Erico House, 93-99 Upper Richmond Road, London SW15 2TG, UK
Phone: (44 20) 8785 5995
Email: info@murdochbooks.co.uk
Web: www.allenandunwin.com
Murdoch Books is a wholly owned division of Allen & Unwin Pty Ltd

A Cataloguing-in-Publication entry is available from the National Library of Australia
www.trove.nla.gov.au
A catalogue record for this book is available from the British Library

ISBN (AUS) 9 781 74331 634 4
ISBN (UK) 978 1 74336 610 3

Cover and text design by Ruth Grüner
Set in 18 pt Hoefler Text by Ruth Grüner
Colour reproduction by Splitting Image, Clayton, Victoria
This book was printed in January 2015 at Hang Tai Printing (Guang Dong) Ltd.,
Xin Cheng Ind Est, Xie Gang Town, Dong Guan, Guang Dong Province, China.

1 3 5 7 9 10 8 6 4 2

traceballa.yolasite.com

With thanks to Susi Blue